·The Prologue·

Most of the Britons in Novocastrum were quite
happy being part of the Roman Empire.
Everybody knew the emperor was mad, bad, and a
complete idiot, but at least he was far away in Rome...

Then, one autumn, AD66 it was, I think, things
began to change. The revolt began on quite a small
scale. Someone threw a turnip at a centurion.
Protesters lay down in front of the governor's chariot.
(That rebellion was quickly squashed!)
People started to whisper nasty things about
the way us Romans wrote our numbers...

Cora and I thought the protests would soon die
down, but they didn't. They got worse. And there was
one very good reason: a statue of Minerva, goddess
of war, had been seen walking through the local
temple, telling people to rise up against Rome!

A walking, talking, living statue! This sounded just
the job for two toga-clad detectives...

·THE CAST·

(In order of personal hygiene.)

ANTONIUS PANTONIUS (Ant)

Private detective.
Given a detective agency
by his uncle. Not sure
whether he likes the job or
area – or his cousin, Cora.

CORA DECORUM (Dec)

Ant's partner. She quite likes
the idea of being a detective.

SUETONIUS CURTIS

Roman number II.
Slimy number I.

MAXIMUS RESPECTUS (Mad Max)

Big cheese in the
Roman army. It's hard to
pull the wool over his eye.

GAN (Ex-gladiator)

Gan the gladiator.
He turned losing into
an art form.

·CONTENTS·

She's Plastered!

Gan, the ex-gladiator, burst through our front curtain. He was out of breath.

"Hurry! You have to come quick! Before it goes!"

I flung on a cloak and called to Cora. She was reading a letter from her father and said she'd follow us as soon as she'd finished.

"Where exactly are we going?"
"The temple," wheezed Gan.
"Now, come on!"

Gan used to be one of the most famous gladiators in Wallsend. A one-armed ex-bandit with a bad case of cowardice, Gan had lost more contests than anyone else in the history of the games. Including once, famously, against two kittens from Barnsley. Now he was retired and living quietly up north... Or at least he was supposed to be!

Hey, slow down old chum!

I hadn't been to the temple for a few days and was surprised at the change. Crowds of angry locals had gathered outside, it was so busy we could hardly get up the steps.

9

I was quite glad I'd arrived with Gan, who was built like the back end of the Coliseum.* Romans didn't seem to be exactly flavour of the month.

*Roman version of Wembley stadium.

Gan drove a path through the crowds like Boudicca* on her driving test.

*Well-known British queen (and dodgy driver). Gives us Romans a hard time.

After what seemed like an age, a priestess showed us through to the temple and we each made our own tribute to the Goddess Minerva.

Squashed dandelion

(It wasn't much of a tribute, but then it had been a bad month for business.)

The temple itself was dark and airy. On either side, scented candles were lit, and torches flickered on the walls.

There were hundreds of people inside. I hadn't seen it so busy since the last SlaveZone* concert.

*Roman boy band. Not my cup of hemlock.

Gan motioned me to a bench by the main altar.

"Wait until you see this," he whispered.

My eyes strained in the darkness. In this kind of light I'd have struggled to see one of Hannibal's elephants.

Gan pointed to the giant statue of Minerva. The one with lots of snakes writhing round her head.

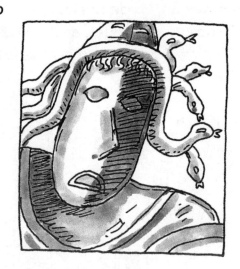

I looked again. Squinting my eyes. He was right! The great stone and plaster monument – it must have been ten metres tall – had begun to move from side to side.

"And the eyes...look at the eyes!" said Gan.

They had begun to glow. Red...the colour of anger!

Minerva, goddess of war and wisdom, was lurching slowly towards us. The effect was quite terrifying, a great groan went up from the other worshippers. I had an odd feeling in my stomach.

"And now..." Gan whispered, "...and now, she speaks!"

"What? The statue *talks*?!" I hissed.

"Shhh!"

2

Ant Almost Gets Fired

"I AM THE GODDESS MINERVA!"
All around us people were bowing down, sobbing, trembling...

I have come to tell you, native people of Novacastrum... That it is time you rose up and threw out those Romans!

I couldn't believe it! A Roman goddess inside a Roman temple telling the Britons to throw us out!

The statue was still moving forwards. It was heading our way. I quickly decided I'd seen enough and leapt up from the bench. Unfortunately I collided with a Pict who'd just had the same idea.

THWACK!

Our heads knocked together and I fell to the ground. (Picts are much harder headed than Romans.)

Minerva's giant statue was now only a few metres away. Her red eyes blazed in the darkness. I felt their fiery gaze upon me...

I felt Gan grab hold of my toga and pull me out from under the statue.

Not a moment too soon! A jet of flame shot out from Minerva's mouth and scorched the spot I'd been lying on. That lady's breath was hotter than a spicy kebab! And it was *me* who'd have been roasted...

With Gan's help I managed to fight my way out of the temple and down the steps to where Cora had just arrived in her mum's chariot.

The angry mob tore at our heels, but thanks to some smart driving from Cora we were able to make our escape. We left behind a piece of my best cloak, and a mob baying for our blood.

On our return to the office I went to water the horses whilst Gan filled Cora in on all the details.

Gan was very concerned for our safety. He was going back up north and asked if we'd like to join him there until the situation improved.

Thanks, Gan, but I'm sure we'll be OK. Most of the trouble seems to be centred around the temple.

You know where I am if you need me. Good luck.

Gan went home and we fastened the front curtain tightly behind him. It wasn't until lunchtime that we had another visitor. A very unexpected visitor.

3

Me? An Enemy?

Suetonius Curtis's* glass eye always made me feel a little queasy, especially just after lunch. (But then so did his normal one. Maybe he was just a queasy kind of guy.)

Hail Rome!

*Number two in the Roman army in Wallsend. To dig the dirt on this all-round nasty piece of work, read GLADIATORS!

"You two have a good reputation for sniffing out troublemakers," he announced, in his usual whining voice. "You managed to help me once before, and now I find I have to turn to you again."

Don't sound too keen!

...I suppose as loyal Romans you have heard that the natives are growing restless?

Yes, but...

We have to put a stop to it. Captain Maximus feels we shouldn't use force. Which is a great pity. I think force can be fun...

He cracked a nut with his fingers and threw the shell on to the floor. (Cheek!)

...We know the trouble is coming from a talking statue located in the temple of Minerva.

He gave me a look I didn't like.

Really?

Now, I'm as superstitious as the next Roman, who is you as it happens. But something fishy is going on. Find out what is happening and report to me.

But the temple... Any Roman going near that place will be...

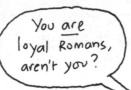

You are loyal Romans, aren't you?

We nodded.

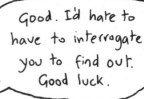

Good. I'd hate to have to interrogate you to find out. Good luck.

He left, with a little smirk on his lips, surrounded by two burly bouncers I recognised from the Ben Hur nightclub.

"I hate him!" glowered Cora, when our visitor had gone. She was sweeping up a large pile of nut shells he'd managed to drop on to the floor.

Me too, but I guess we'll have to take the case. Suetonius would make a very dangerous enemy...

Got any ideas how to get back inside the temple without being torn to pieces?

The Weather Warcast

4

The temple was never closed, not even at night, so getting in without anyone seeing us wasn't going to be easy. Cora knew of a route beneath the streets, using drainage pipes from the public baths.

I used to sneak out of the villa when I was a teenager by using this tunnel...

We had to crouch all the way, bent double, but I suppose it was small price to pay for not getting massacred by a rioting mob.

THE WEATHER WARCAST
With Miklos Pisces

When we reached the end of the tunnel. Cora
handed me some priestess's robes and told me
to put them on.

The temple was much quieter than before. A few of the priestesses walked airily around, keeping the candles lit and the incense burning. In the distance, I could see the statue. The memory of our last meeting flashed into my mind. Fortunately this time there was no fire in its eyes. (Phew!)

Had that huge piece of stone and plaster really moved? And why did Minerva have it in for us Romans? Perhaps our sacrifices hadn't been up to the mark? I put a nice bag of salted nuts on to the altar.

We should get closer. I'd like to see if there are any tracks or wires around.

Cora and I flitted through the shadows to get a closer view of the statue. It was standing in its normal spot.

A couple of shadowy figures had suddenly appeared next to the statue.

"The door is stuck!" hissed one of them.

"Well give it a tug, you fool!"

That last voice seemed very familiar, even in the echoing gloom. For a second, the light from one of the torches illuminated his figure.

Svetonius Curtis!

What was he doing down there?

There was a small entrance at the base
of the statue. The first figure slipped inside.
"I can't move it on my own!"
came a muffled voice
from within.

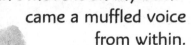

Weakling!

You try parading
a statue up and
down for twenty
minutes and see
how you get on...

Do you have
that speech
I gave you?

Yes, I have
it here.

There was no doubt about it. Suetonius was up to his glass eyeball in the mystery of the talking statue. But I couldn't see why he'd want to encourage the Britons to rise up against Rome. Or why he'd told us to come to the temple...

Someone had seen us...

The priestess's alarm in turn alerted Suetonius and his companion.

I glanced quickly across at Cora, we both knew what to do.

Two guards had emerged
to block our escape route.

I was glad Gan
had taught me a few
of his more successful
gladiator moves.

The underground exit was before us. Cora went first. I tried to keep the guards at bay. A sword swished past my shoulder.

I leapt into the darkness, landing on Cora's toe. "Owww!"

And then we ran. How we ran!

For a while steps seemed to echo behind us. If we were caught in here it would be a slaughter...

5

Council Of War

Maximus Respectus, captain of the Roman garrison, arrived with ten guards at his side. They found it hard to fit into our office.

I knew Maximus through Cora's uncle. He didn't much like the idea of private detectives. He said it would never catch on. But to give him his due, when we sent our note informing him we had news of a traitor in his camp, he'd come at once.

He listened patiently to our story about the talking statue, and about Suetonius Curtis being the man behind it all. Then he rose to his feet (usually the best place to rise to). He only said two words:

6

Someone Slips Up!

Maximus Respectus looked even less like a priestess than I did, but disguise was important if our plan was to work.

This is madness!

We'd been busy all morning, polishing the temple floor with turtle wax.

We stood back and examined the floor. It gleamed as brightly as a legionnaire's sword.

A gong sounded. People were beginning to enter the temple. We retreated to the shadows to await events.

The temple didn't take long to fill. There was an excited atmosphere. No one could wait to see what Minerva would say next. Many of the Britons were armed, just waiting, it seemed, for Minerva's orders.

The snake-strewn head of the statue turned once more from side to side. Even though I knew it to be a trick, it was still a frightening sight. Her eyes began to glow...

Even Maximus, who had seen many battles, and been married for thirty years, was taken aback.

The gods have mercy on us!

Slowly, terrifyingly, Minerva began to sway forwards.

Britons! Now is the time to take up arms against the Romans and their cruel leader. Drive him out! Drive out Maximus!

"Drive out Maximus!" repeated the crowd, as though in a trance.

The statue had finally reached the section of marble floor we'd been polishing. That piece of floor was now as slippery as a Goth's armpit on a hot day.

The statue began to wobble, and then it started to slide. It slid for a couple of metres, then began to lean over. The lights in the eyes went out and smoke started pouring out from its ears.

Finally, losing its grip altogether, it came crashing to the ground. Inside the temple there was chaos... Some froze, others ran to the statue. The priestesses huddled together in tears. Maximus Respectus was on his feet, he ordered his legionnaires forward from out of the shadows.

Minerva lay on her side, broken into three or four pieces. Seen from underneath, the statue was completely hollow. From inside the secret compartment came crawling Suetonius Curtis and a couple of dazed accomplices. He was still in fighting mood.

"Fight back, you fools!" he shouted to the crowds.

> I'll help you... Together we can beat these Romans!

But faced by Maximus's troops, and seeing that the talking statue was nothing but a fraud, the Britons began to melt away.

Maximus gave me a big hug followed by a Roman salute.

He saluted Cora too.

Suetonius Curtis was led away. I had to feel a little sorry for him, despite everything. He was heading for a lunch appointment with some hungry lions in the Millennium Drome...

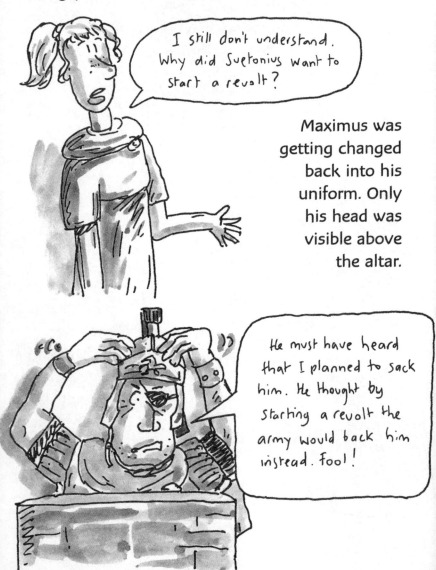

Maximus was getting changed back into his uniform. Only his head was visible above the altar.

I still couldn't work out why he would ask us to investigate his own plot.

Because you gave him the perfect alibi. He could convince me that he was trying to stamp out the trouble. The only mistake he made is that you two are smarter than you look!

Was that a compliment?! Compliments are all very well, but they don't pay the grocery bills... Then Maximus told us the good news: we'd be getting a sizeable reward for our help.

The temple was now almost deserted. The only other people left were the priestesses, now busy sweeping up pieces of statue. They said they would build another one soon... One with no secret compartments!

We said our prayers and left.

Strange To Relate

It was freezing outside, and I was glad of the warmth from the fire. Cora came and sat beside me on the couch.

She looked serious, very serious, considering we'd just solved an important case.

I looked up from the book I'd been reading.*

*HANDSOME NERO MAKES A GREAT JOB OF RUNNING ROME by er, Nero.

This was a bit of a bolt from the blue, and I couldn't think of what to say. As usual, Cora was taking it all in her stride.

She got up and walked to the window. It was a fine, starry night.

A fine, starry night ↳

My real parents were lost trying to cross the Alps in a chariot.

What a way to go!

So Cora wasn't my cousin, after all. How strange! (I hadn't seen that one coming.)

"So that means we're not cousins, just partners...
in crime," she added, with a certain sparkle in
her eyes.

Ludicra, a batty fortune-teller, once predicted
that Cora and I would become an item.* Maybe
the old girl had finally got something right.

*For all the gory details, read FLYING SORCERESS.

There was a knock at the curtain. Cora drew it back and there stood a standard-bearer from the Roman Army.

"You two private detectives?" he asked.
I nodded.

Missing legion? What a job!
Any thoughts of romance were
going to have to go on the back
incense burner! (Phew!)

Clueless about
what to read next?

Why not track
down these books by
Keith Brumpton!

ROME AND AWAY

☐ **1 Gladiators!**   ISBN 1 86039 920 7   £3.99

☐ **2 Flying Sorceress**   ISBN 1 86039 922 3   £3.99

☐ **3 Chariots on Fire!**   ISBN 1 86039 924 X   £3.99

☐ **4 Statue of Terror**   ISBN 1 86039 926 6   £3.99

DEREK THE DEPRESSED VIKING

☐ **1 Who'd be a Viking?**

ISBN 1 86039 600 3   £3.99

☐ **2 The Dragon from the Black Lagoon**

ISBN 1 86039 601 1   £3.99

☐ **3 Kidnapped by Ice Maidens**

ISBN 1 86039 602 X   £3.99

☐ **4 Nice Throne, Shame About the Crown**

ISBN 1 86039 603 8   £3.99

Keith Brumpton's books are available from all good bookshops,
or can be ordered direct from the publisher:
Orchard Books, PO BOX 29, Douglas IM99 1BQ
Credit card orders please telephone 01624 836000 or fax 01624 837033
or e-mail: bookshop@enterprise.net for details.

To order please quote title, author and ISBN and your full name
and address. Cheques and postal orders should be made payable to
'Bookpost plc'. Postage and packing is FREE within the UK
(overseas customers should add £1.00 per book).

Prices and availability are subject to change.